Contents

Chapter 1
Meeting Grandfather

Heidi felt cross and tired as Aunt Dete pulled her up the steep slope.

"I'd go faster if I wasn't wearing *all* my clothes," said Heidi.

"You'll need them at your grandfather's and I don't want to carry them," said her aunt, angrily.

"Do you think Grandfather will want me?" Heidi asked nervously.

Aunt Dete shook her head. "I don't know. He's a miserable old man and he hasn't seen you since you were a baby. But I've taken care of you for long enough. Now it's his turn."

At last they reached
Grandfather's hut, at the
very top of the mountain.
Dete rapped sharply on
the door. It creaked
open and an old
man peered out.

"What do you want?"
he asked, gruffly.

5

"This is your granddaughter, Heidi," Dete explained. "Your dead son's child. I've brought her to live with you."

"I don't want her," said the old man, trying to shut the door.

"I don't care," Dete snapped. "You have to take her. Both her parents are dead. I've found a good job in Frankfurt and she can't come with me."

With that,
Heidi's aunt turned
and ran down the mountain.

Grandfather stared silently at Heidi. Heidi stared back.

"He doesn't want me," she thought, sadly, "but where else can I go?"

"Well... you'd better come in," said Grandfather, with a scowl.

Heidi stepped into the hut and looked around. There didn't seem to be room for her anywhere.

"Where shall I sleep?" she asked. Grandfather shrugged. He didn't even look at her. "You'll have to find your own bed," he growled.

Heidi looked again and saw a ladder in the corner. Feeling curious, she climbed up into a hayloft. From the window, she could see a green valley far below and hear pine trees whooshing in the wind.

She lifted some of the sweet-smelling hay, puffing it up into the shape of a mattress. "I'll sleep here," she called. "It's lovely!"

"She shows some sense," Grandfather muttered to himself. "Come down now," he ordered. "It's time for supper."

Heidi watched Grandfather blow onto the embers of the fire, making the flames blaze. Fetching a bowl, he filled it to the brim with rich, creamy milk.

"Here you are," he said.
Then he toasted bread and cheese over the fire until they were a glorious golden brown.

12

Delicious smells filled the hut and Heidi realized how hungry she was. She licked up oozing drips of cheese, crunched the toast and drank the milk to the last drop.

Through the open door, she saw the sky and mountainside glow in the setting sun. "I like it here, Grandfather," she said.

Good night, Heidi.

That night, Heidi snuggled down in the hayloft. As she fell asleep she wondered why Grandfather lived all alone, high on the mountain. What had happened to make him so sad and unfriendly?

Chapter 2

The goat boy

Early next morning, Heidi woke to
the sound of bells. She sat up.
Sunshine poured through the
hayloft window, turning her straw
bed into shimmering gold.

Quickly, she dressed and shot down the ladder. A boy was standing at the door, whistling.

"This is Peter, the goat boy," Grandfather told her. "He's come for Little Swan and Little Bear."

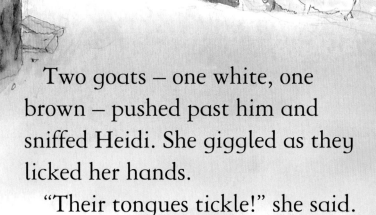

Two goats – one white, one brown – pushed past him and sniffed Heidi. She giggled as they licked her hands.

"Their tongues tickle!" she said.

"Do you want to come with me?"
Peter shouted over the bleats and
bells. "I'm going up the mountain to
find fresh grass for them."

"Can I?" Heidi asked Grandfather.

"I suppose," he replied. "But have
your breakfast first." He sat on a
stool and milked Little Bear, then
handed Heidi a bowl of fresh milk.

"Come on!" said Peter, as soon as she'd finished. "You can stay at the back and make sure none of the goats get lost."

As they ran over rocks to the mountain pastures, Peter showed Heidi the mountain's secrets.

He pointed to an eagle's nest hidden in the craggy peaks and the spots where wild flowers grew. The mountain looked as if a giant had scattered handfuls of jewels over it.

Heidi had never seen so many flowers. She picked great blue and yellow bunches for Grandfather.

Every day, Heidi went out with Peter and the goats. And every day, her cheeks grew rosier and her eyes more sparkly. Grandfather fed her crusty bread, tasty cheese and Little Swan's milk. At night, he told her stories by the fire.

Heidi had never been happier...
until one morning, when the door
flew open and there stood Aunt
Dete in a brand new dress.

"I've come for Heidi," she
announced. "I should never have
left her with you in the first place."

"No," cried Heidi, suddenly
afraid. "I like it here. I want to
stay with Grandfather."

Dete ignored her. "I've found a place for Heidi in Frankfurt," she told Grandfather. "Clara Sesemann, a little girl who's always ill, wants a friend to keep her company."

"If Heidi behaves," her aunt went on, "Mr. Sesemann will pay her and buy her some fine new clothes. It's a great chance for her."

Grandfather had been looking crosser and crosser during this speech. "Take her and spoil her then!" he bellowed at Dete. "But don't bother coming back. Ever!"

Just go!

Ignoring Heidi's protests, Dete gripped her arm and dragged her outside. As they left, Heidi saw Grandfather sitting alone, his head in his hands.

"Poor Grandfather!" cried Heidi, tears trickling down her face.

"Come *on*, Heidi," said Dete, pushing her down the mountain. "I'm sorry I ever left you with that sad old man."

"Why is he so sad?" asked Heidi.

"He thinks the world is a bad place," her aunt replied. "First, his wife died. Then your father, his only child, wasted all his money and died too. But your grandfather's just made things worse for himself."

"He said there was only misery in the world and shut himself away up here. Forget him Heidi. Think about Frankfurt."

"I'll never forget him!" cried
Heidi.

"It's for your own good," Dete
declared, striding off.

Heidi was quiet, but secretly she
made a promise. "One day I'll
come back to him."

Chapter 3

Heidi and Clara

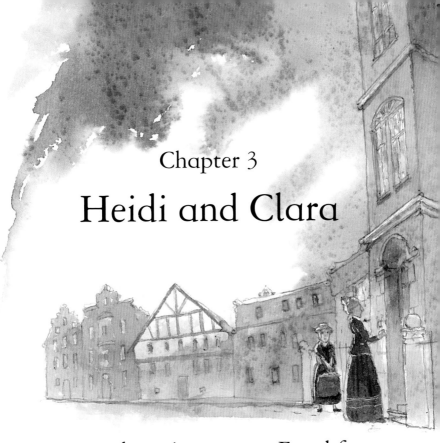

It was a long journey to Frankfurt. The sun was beginning to set when they stopped before a grand house in a cobbled street. Dete pulled the bell. "This is it," she muttered.

A well-dressed servant opened the door and led them into a vast hall.

Heidi felt very small and shabby.
She felt even worse when the
housekeeper, Mrs. Rotenmeyer,
saw her.

"You look most unsuitable,"
she said to Heidi with a sigh.
"I suppose you'd better
meet Clara."

Clara lay on a heap of pillows in
a frilly four-poster bed. Her face
was pale and the room was hot.

"Thank you for coming, Heidi," she said, quietly. "I'll like having company. I can't get out of bed."

"Why not?" asked Heidi.

"I've been sick and I'm still weak," Clara explained. "I don't think I'll ever get better."

"No one could get better in this hot, stuffy room," Heidi thought. She ran over to a window and flung it wide open.

The street below jostled with people, horses and carriages. Heidi could hear strange music mixed in with the clattering hooves and footsteps.

That'll cheer Clara up!

Leaning out, she saw a ragged boy with a street organ. A pair of kittens peeked out of his pockets.

Heidi rushed downstairs and onto the street. "Can you come here?" she called, beckoning him over. "There's someone I want you to play for."

Moments later, they were both bounding up the stairs.

"Surprise!" shouted Heidi, throwing open Clara's door and letting in the ragged boy.

Downstairs, Mrs. Rotenmeyer the housekeeper was puzzled. She could hear singing, laughing, music, even kittens – and all coming from Clara's bedroom.

"What's going on in here?" she shrieked, as she stormed into Clara's room.

"How did this dreadful boy get in?" she demanded. "I blame you," she said, glaring at Heidi. "I knew you were trouble from the moment I saw you. Go to your room at once."

"No," pleaded Clara. "Heidi was only trying to cheer me up." She held Heidi's hand. "Please don't send Heidi to her room. We want to have our supper together."

There was nothing Mrs. Rotenmeyer could do. She had to obey Clara. "All right," she said crossly, turning to go, "but get that dirty boy out of here now!"

Mrs. Rotenmeyer returned carrying a tray loaded with rich food. Greasy chunks of meat swam in a cream sauce. Clara pushed it around her plate and hardly ate anything. Heidi didn't like it either.

"I don't get hungry lying in bed," Clara murmured.

"You'd soon get hungry running up the mountain to Grandfather's hut," Heidi told her.

Clara looked sad. "But since I've been ill, I can't walk."

"That's terrible," said Heidi.

The warm room and heavy meal were making her feel sleepy. She had to go outside to breathe some fresh air. Stale smells hung over the noisy street.

Heidi longed for the cool clear air of the mountain and the soft breeze that made the pine trees rustle.

Some time after Heidi's arrival, the servants started claiming the house was haunted by a ghost.

"A white figure floats down the stairs at night," said a maid.

The servants were so upset, Mrs. Rotenmeyer grew worried. "I must tell Clara's father," she decided.

Mr. Sesemann only laughed when he heard the news. "There's no such thing as ghosts," he said. "I'll catch your ghost to prove it."

38

The next night he waited in the
hall at the bottom of the stairs.
Heidi came down, wearing a
white nightgown. She tried
to open the locked front
door, then sobbed.

Mr. Sesemann went over to her
and saw she was still fast asleep.

"Heidi has been sleepwalking," Mr. Sesemann explained to Clara and Mrs. Rotenmeyer, the next morning. "The poor child is so homesick, her dreams felt real. I think she'd better go home."

Chapter 4

Heidi goes home

The following week, Grandfather looked out of the window and could hardly believe his eyes. A peculiar procession was stumbling up the mountain slope.

Two men were struggling with suitcases. A third hauled a wheelchair and a fourth carried a child bundled up in a shawl. The men puffed and panted, their shirts drenched in sweat.

Ahead of them all danced Heidi.

She raced up the slope and threw herself into Grandfather's arms.

"Heidi!" he cried. "You've come back to me."

"I missed you," Heidi said. "Look, Mr. Sesemann has written you a letter to explain."

Dear Sir,

Heidi was too homesick to stay with us but Clara could not bear to say goodbye. I hope you will forgive me for sending her with Heidi to stay for a month.

Clara, alas, is still very weak after a long illness. She has no appetite and cannot walk. I hope her visit to you on the mountain will give her new strength.

With all my thanks and best wishes,

Yours sincerely,

Hans Sesemann

Grandfather turned to Clara. "I'm very pleased to meet you," he said. "And thank you for bringing Heidi back to me. You'll soon feel better breathing our mountain air."

Grandfather put Clara's wheelchair in the sunshine, so she could see the wonderful view, and gave her a bowl of fresh milk.

"Guess who really gave you the milk?" Heidi teased, bringing Little Swan over. The goat butted Clara gently, until she realized Little Swan wanted to be stroked.

Clara drank thirstily. "This tastes much nicer than Frankfurt milk," she said.

"Heidi?" came a shout. Peter ran up the path to them. "I heard you were back," he said to Heidi.

"Come out with me tomorrow," he urged her.

"Peter, I can't," said Heidi. "I have to stay with Clara."

Peter gave Clara a jealous look.

"You go Heidi," Clara insisted.

I'll be fine.

I'll pick you some flowers.

All the same, when they set off next morning, Clara looked sad.

"I'll be quick," Heidi promised. "I just want to climb the ridge where the biggest, bluest flowers grow."

Clara watched them go longingly. She would have given anything to be running with them, with strong legs that could skip and jump.

"I wish you'd come," Heidi told Clara when she returned. "We watched an eagle soar above our heads and did somersaults down the mountain."

Clara sighed.

"Cheer up," Grandfather said, trying to comfort her. "The sun has already brought roses to your cheeks. I'm sure you'll soon feel stronger."

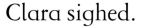

I won't leave you again.

Oh, I wish I could walk...

From where he stood, high on the mountain, Peter could see Heidi and Clara talking together. His heart burned with jealousy.

"I wish that girl hadn't come," he thought. "Heidi's *my* friend. I'll *make* Clara go home." And a plan began to form in his mind.

Chapter 5
Peter's plan

Before sunrise next morning, Peter crept to Grandfather's hut. All was quiet and still.

Just as Peter hoped, Clara's wheelchair stood by the door. Noiselessly, he pushed it to the edge of the mountain and rolled it over a steep, stony cliff.

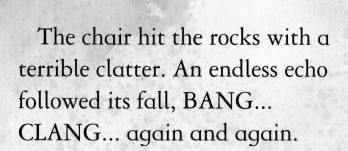

The chair hit the rocks with a terrible clatter. An endless echo followed its fall, BANG... CLANG... again and again.

Peering over the cliff, Peter saw the jagged rocks had smashed the wheelchair into a thousand pieces. Peter looked at what he had done... and fled.

When he arrived at the hut for the goats, Heidi told Peter about Clara's chair. "The wind must have caught it," she said. "Grandfather has to carry Clara everywhere."

"Then Clara will have to go home, won't she?" Peter demanded.

"Aha," murmured Grandfather. "I think I know who blew that puff of wind."

Heidi was shocked. "Did you do it, Peter?" she asked, sharply.

Peter went red. "I'm... I'm sorry," he stammered. "I wanted her to go. You don't have time for me now."

"Peter, you must hate me," said Clara. "You think I've taken Heidi away from you."

"Never mind," Heidi interrupted. "We can all still be friends."

But Grandfather shook his head.

"Mr. Sesemann may not be so forgiving," he said. "Clara's chair is still broken."

"If only Clara could walk..." said Heidi.

"I do feel stronger," Clara whispered. "Perhaps I could try."

She edged herself forward and put her slender feet on the ground. Grandfather gently took hold of her hands and helped her to stand.

"My legs feel so weak," said Clara, trembling.

"Be brave," said Grandfather.

Slowly, Clara put one foot in front of the other.

Clara wobbled, but Grandfather supported her.

"Rest now," he ordered. "You can try again tomorrow."

Every day, Clara walked a little more. Hungry from the exercise and fresh mountain air, she wolfed down huge meals. Strength flowed into her and she tingled with energy. "Won't Father be amazed?" she thought.

Chapter 6

A surprise for Mr. Sesemann

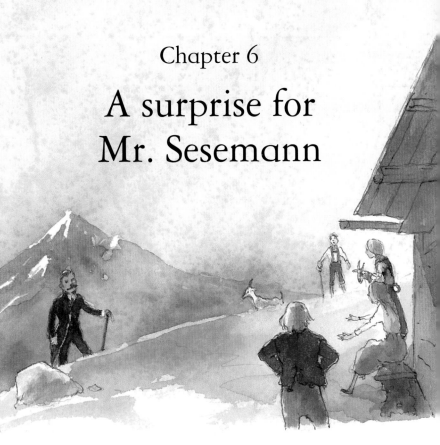

A few weeks later, Mr. Sesemann arrived for Clara. He hardly recognized his daughter with her glowing face, bright eyes and thick, shiny hair.

When Clara stood up, he was astonished and when she walked up to him, he had to sit down.

"Is it really you?" he said. "I can't believe it. You're walking!"

"Isn't it wonderful," laughed Clara. "Grandfather and Heidi made it happen."

"And Peter," Grandfather put in, his eyes twinkling.

"You did it, Clara," said Heidi.
"It was your hard work."

"It's a miracle," Mr. Sesemann
beamed. "Clara, I'm proud of you.
Thank you, thank you everyone."

"You must come back to the mountain whenever you want," Heidi told Clara.

"And you must come to Frankfurt – Peter too," said Clara. "We'll find the ragged boy again and dance."

When Clara and her father had gone, Heidi and Grandfather went outside to watch the sunset. The sky and mountains shone red-gold, just like Heidi's first evening.

"It's beautiful," said Grandfather.

"Once I was sad and lonely," he told Heidi, "but you've made me a happy man."